ORLAND PARK PUBLIC LIBRARY
3 1315 00469 4571

P9-CMS-628

# WHERE THE GIANT SLEEPS

Mem Fox

PICTURES BY Vladimir Radunsky

Harcourt, Inc. ORLANDO AUSTIN NEW YORK SAN DIEGO TORONTO LONDON

a b c d e
1
2
3
4
5
This is where
a b c d e

f g h i j
1
2
3
4
5
the giant sleeps,
f g h i j

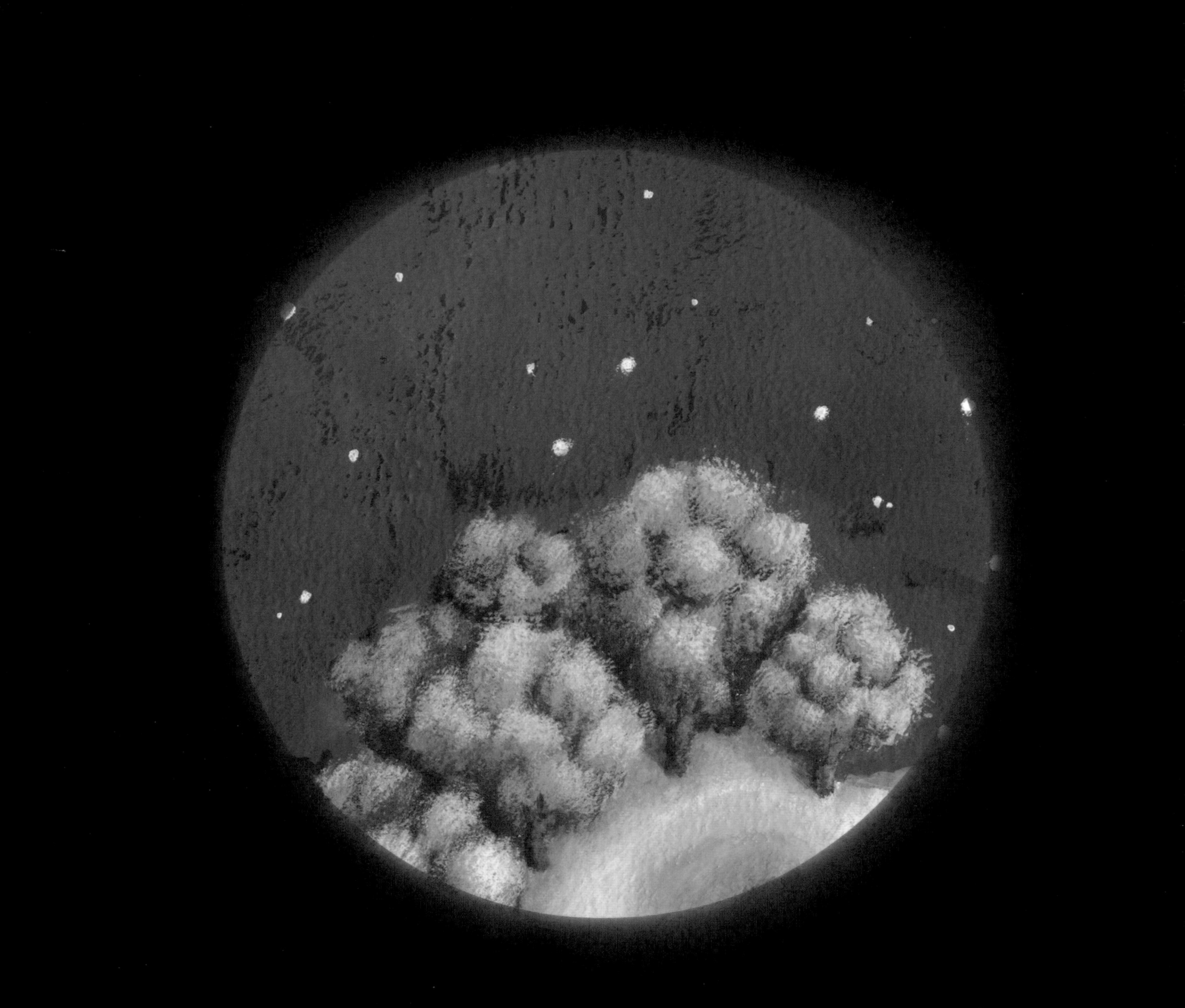

and here the fairy dozes.

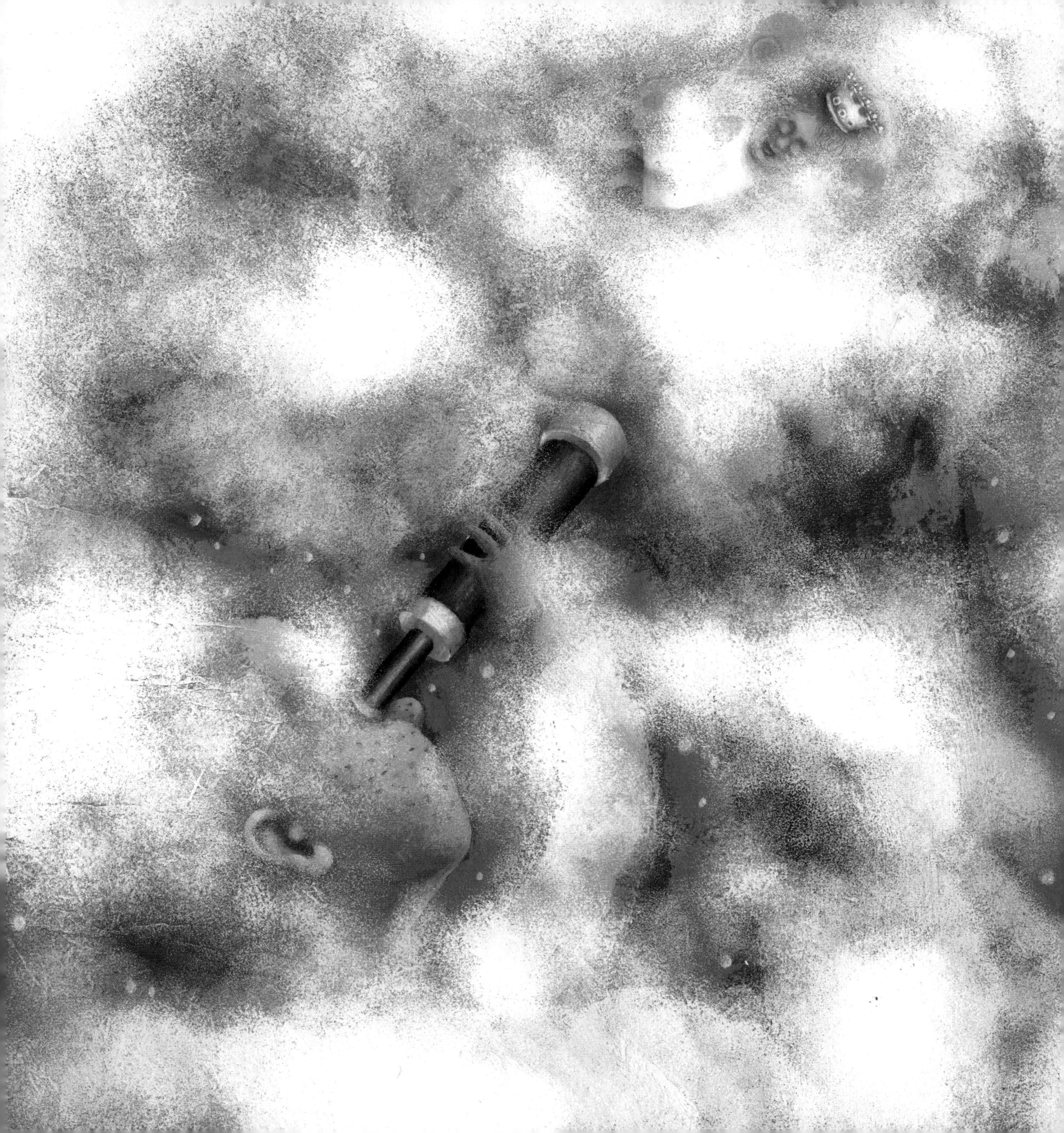

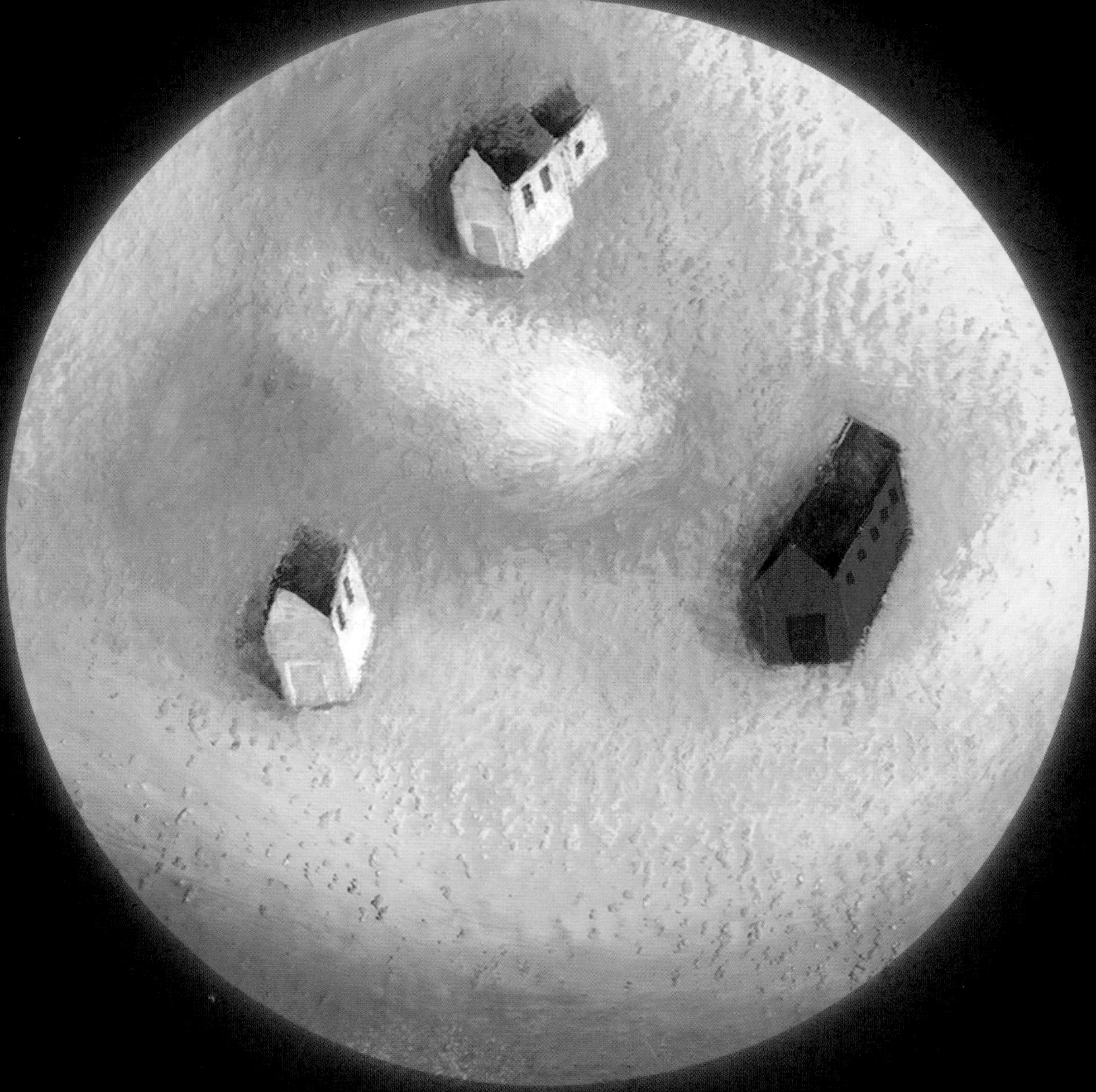

Here the pirate lays his head—
though one eye never closes.

piRAte

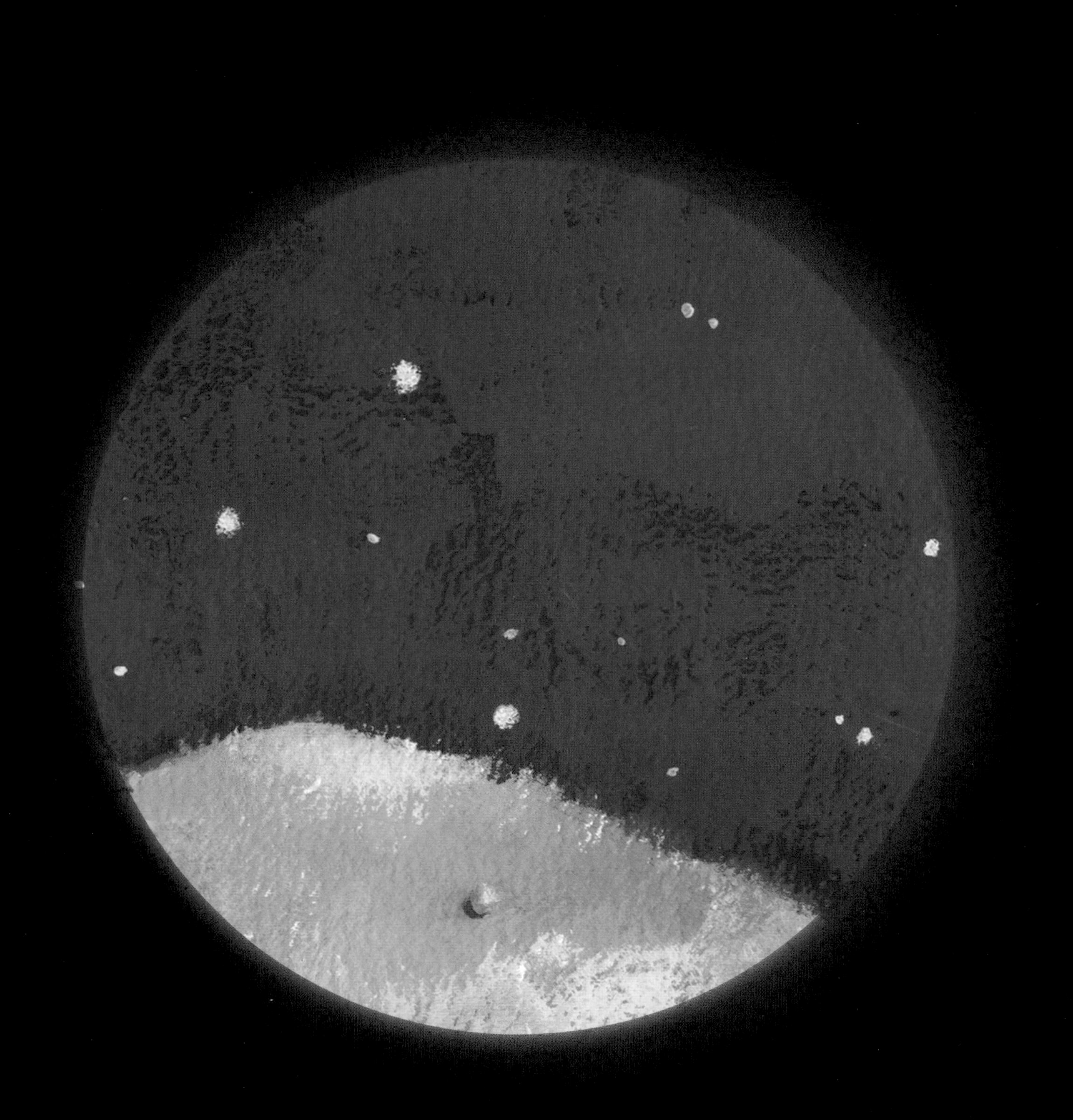

This is where the wizard dreams,

and here lie all the witches.

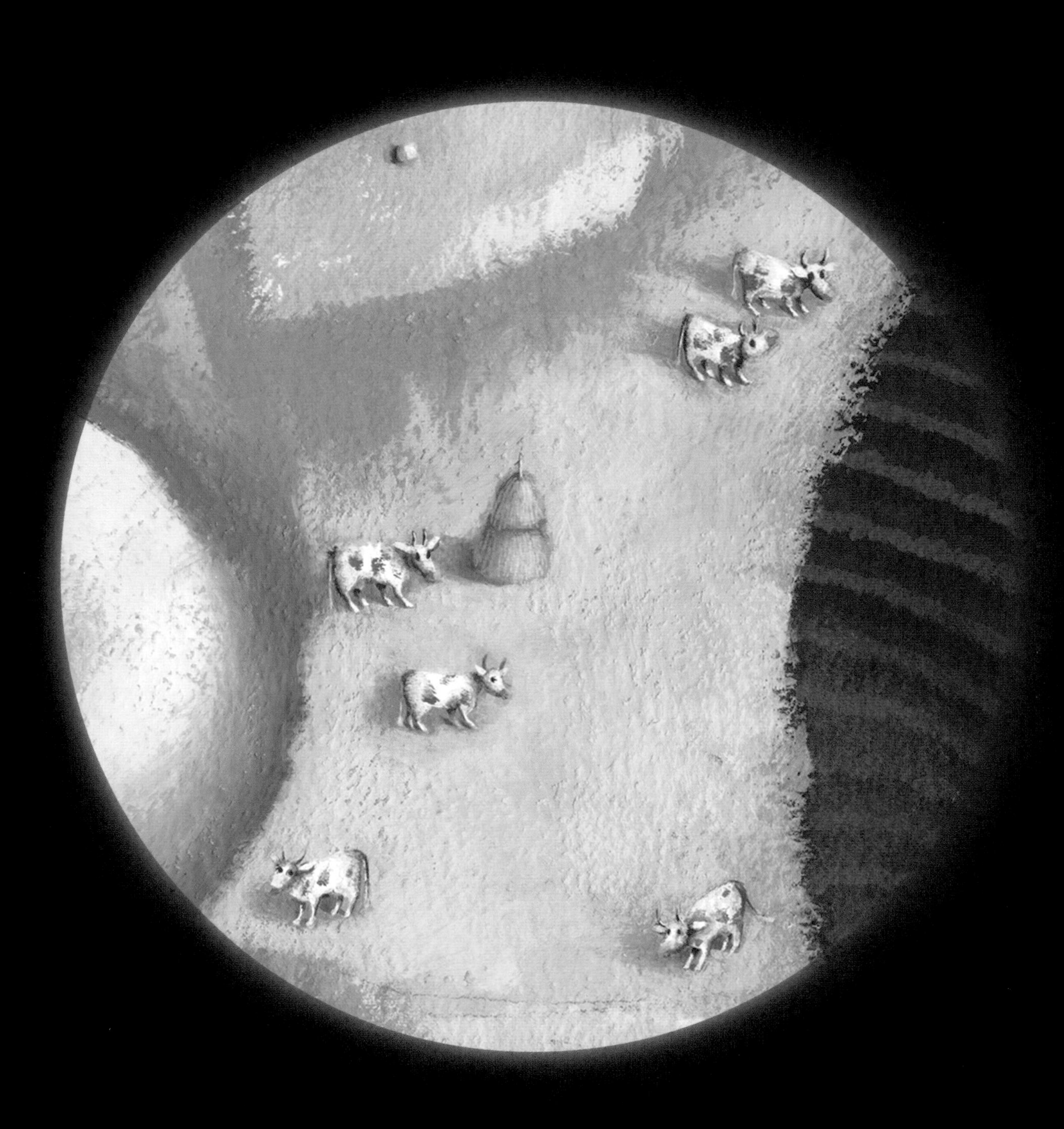

While in a haystack, safe and warm,
a little goblin twitches.

This is where the pixies sleep,
in petals soft and round.

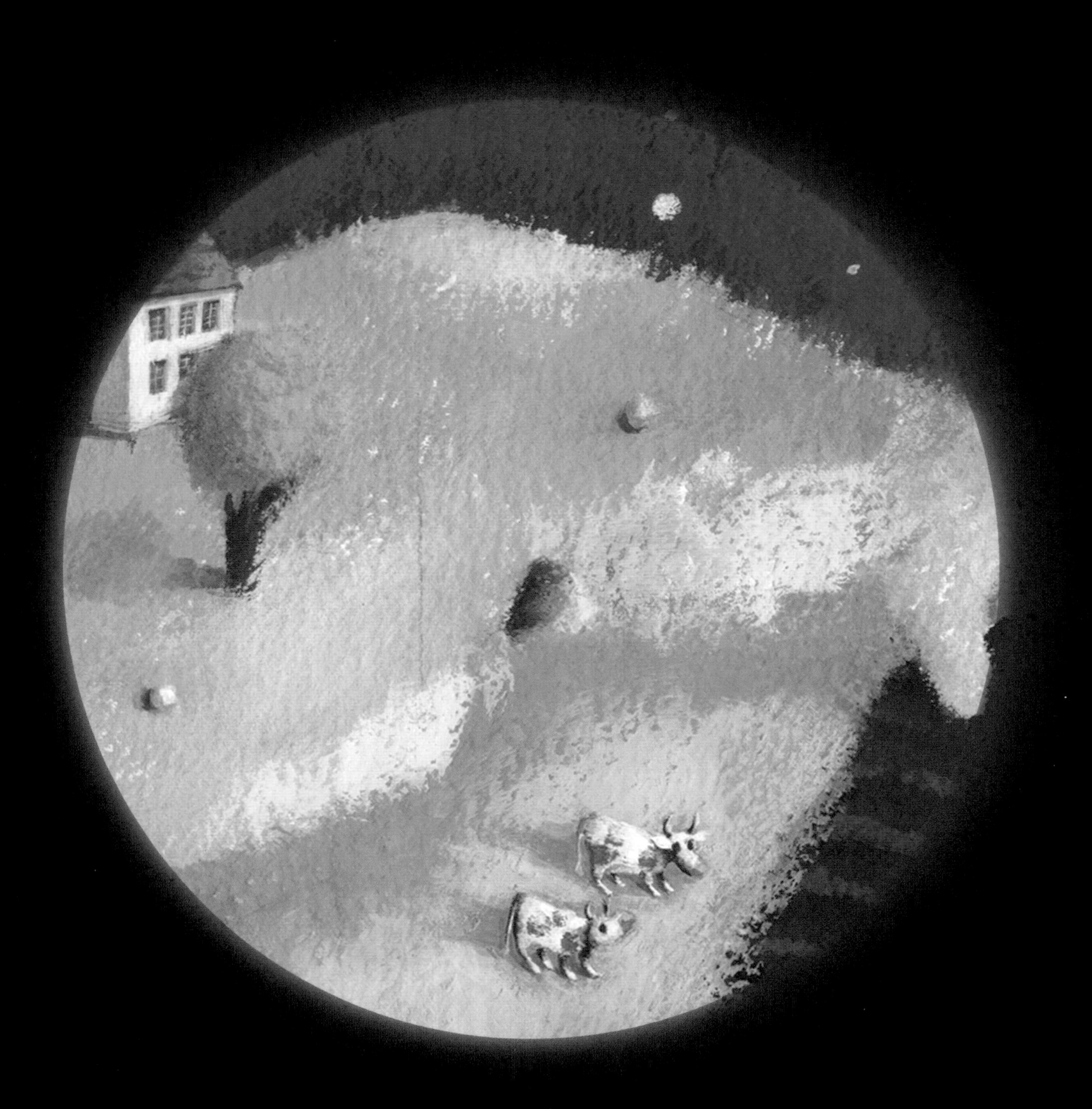

And here the seven dwarfs curl up,
in caves beneath the ground.

Here the dragon lays his head,
breathing fire, and snoring.

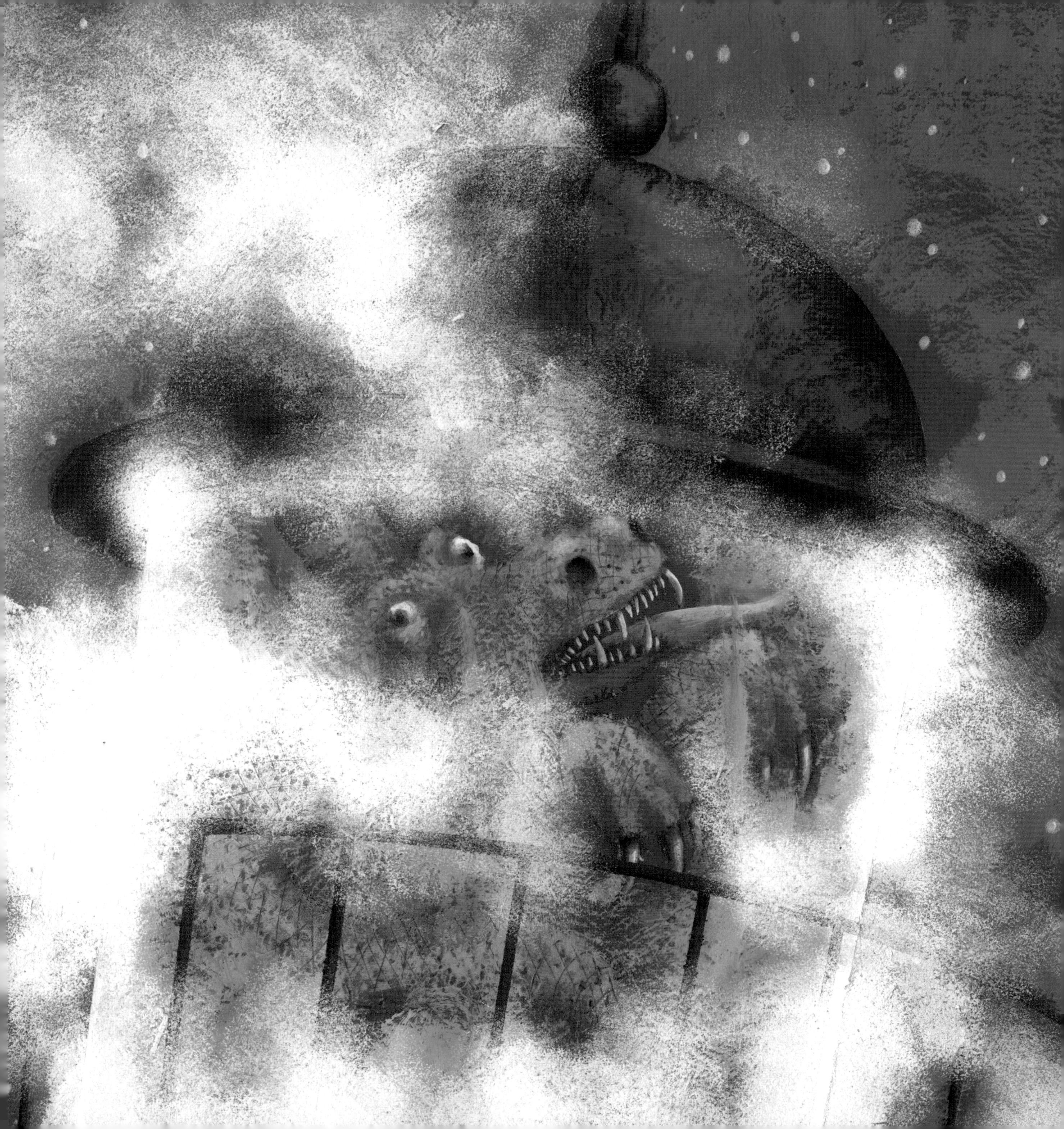

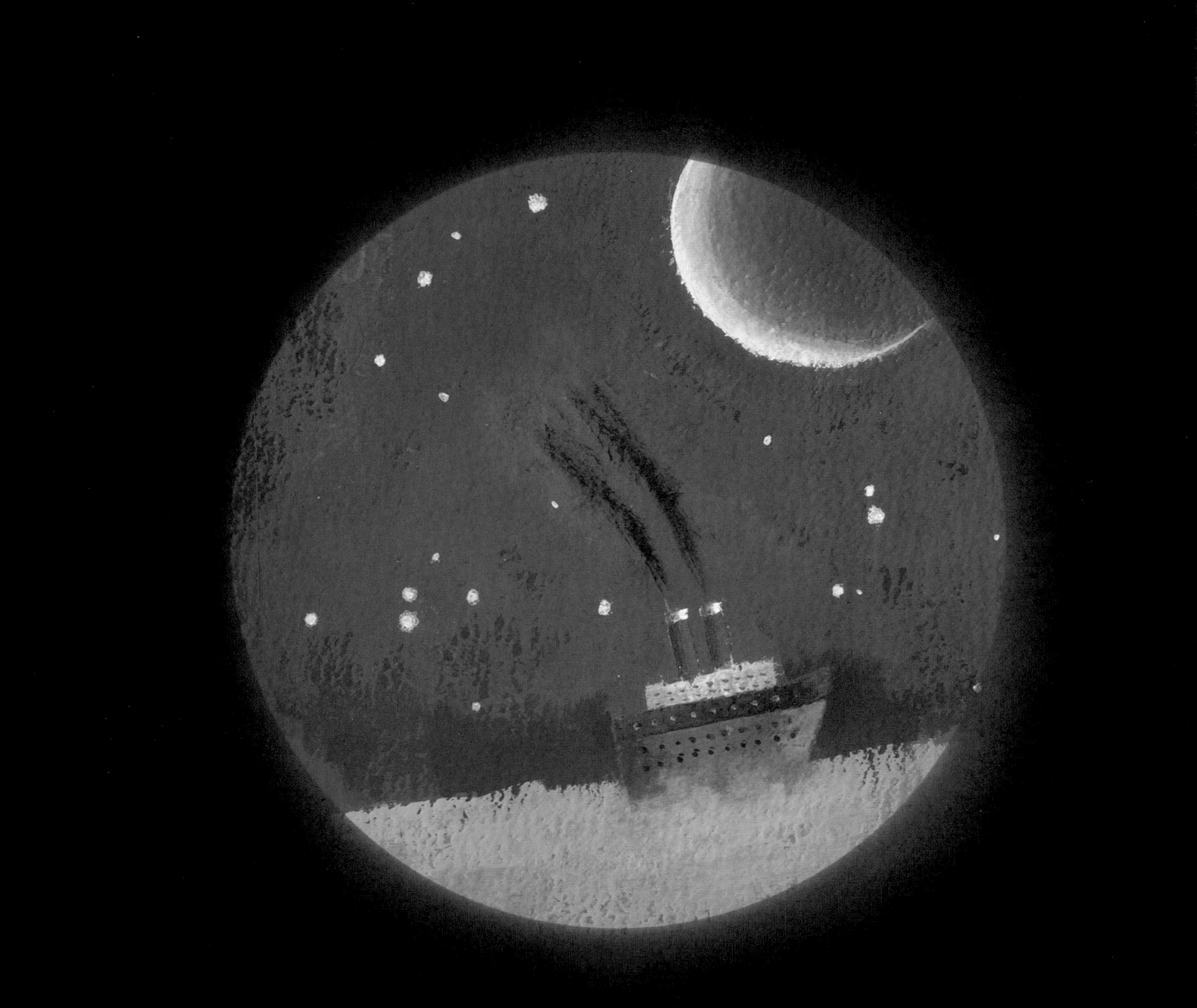

And here the ogre shuts his eyes
and takes a rest from roaring.

But here the elves are wide awake–
sewing with all their might,

WHERE THE GIANT SLEEPS
Mem Fox

to make a quilt of moons and stars
to wrap you in . . . tonight.

For Gordon and Erica – M. F.

To Evgenia, Anna, Sasha, and Kurochka – V. R.





www.HarcourtBooks.com

Library of Congress Cataloging-in-Publication Data: Fox, Mem, 1946- Where the giant sleeps/Mem Fox; illustrated by Vladimir Radunsky. p. cm. Summary: Illustrations and rhyming text portray the different residents of fairyland and where each one goes to sleep. [1. Bedtime—Fiction. 2. Sleep—Fiction. 3. Stories in rhyme.] I. Radunsky, Vladimir, ill. II. Title. PZ8.3.F8245Whm 2007 [E]—dc22 2006020539 ISBN 978-0-15-205785-5

First edition H G F E D C B A

Manufactured in China

The illustrations in this book were done in gouache on handmade paper.

The type was set in Ratbag.

Prepress by Studio Punto Rome.

Color separations by Bright Arts Ltd. Hong Kong

Manufactured by South China Printing Company, Ltd., China

Production supervision by Pascha Gerlinger

Designed by Vladimir Radunsky